The
Three Billy
Goats Gruff

First published in 2007 by
Franklin Watts
338 Euston Road
London
NW1 3BH

Franklin Watts Australia
Level 17/207 Kent Street
Sydney
NSW 2000

A CIP catalogue record for this book is available
from the British Library.

ISBN 978 0 7496 7076 4 (hbk)
ISBN 978 0 7496 7420 5 (pbk)

Series Editor: Melanie Palmer
Series Advisor: Dr Barrie Wade
Series Designer: Peter Scoulding

Printed in China

Franklin Watts is a division of Hachette Children's Books.

For Benjamin and Alexander – W.M.

For Emma and Tom – J.B.

The Three Billy Goats Gruff

by Wes Magee and Julian Burnett

FRANKLIN WATTS

LONDON•SYDNEY

Long ago, there were three Billy
Goats called Gruff.

5

One was small, one was
medium-sized, and one was big.
In spring, the three Billy Goats
Gruff felt hungry.

They decided to climb the
mountain to find the sweet grass.

The Billy Goats Gruff came to a
rushing river with a wooden bridge.
Beneath the bridge lived
an ugly troll.

The troll had a lumpy nose and ears like spears. If anyone tried to cross the bridge he would jump out and gobble them up!

"I'll cross the bridge,"
said the small Billy Goat Gruff.
Tripitty-trap went his small hooves
on the wooden planks.

"Who's crossing my bridge?"
roared the ugly troll.
"Me," said the small Billy Goat.
"I'm hungry."

"So am I," growled the troll.

"And I'm going to gobble you up!"

"But I'm only small," wailed the little goat. "Wait for my brother, he's bigger than me!"

The troll scratched his lumpy nose. "Okay," he growled, and the small goat went *trippity-trap* across the bridge and ran up the mountain.

"I'll cross the bridge," said the medium-sized Billy Goat Gruff. *Trippity-trippity-trap* went his medium-sized hooves on the wooden planks.

"Who's crossing my bridge?"
roared the ugly troll.
"Me," said the medium-sized
Billy Goat. "I'm hungry."

"So am I," growled the troll.
"*Very* hungry, and I'm going
to gobble you up!"

"But I'm only medium-sized,"
wailed the medium-sized Billy Goat.
"Wait for my big brother.
He's much bigger than me!"

The troll scratched his lumpy nose.
"Okay," he growled, and the
medium-sized Billy Goat went
trippity-trippity-trap across the bridge.

21

"I'll cross the bridge," said the big Billy Goat Gruff. *Trippity-trippity-trippity-trap* went his big hooves on the wooden planks.

"Who's crossing my bridge?"
roared the ugly troll.
"Me," said the big goat.
"I'm hungry."

"So am I," growled the troll.
"Very, *very* hungry, and I'm going
to gobble you up!" The troll
jumped onto the bridge,
showing his sharp teeth.

The big Billy Goat Gruff lowered
his big horns and charged at the
ugly troll. He butted him in
the middle of his fat tummy.
With a cry, the troll went up
 into the air.

SPLASH! The troll fell into the
rushing river and was swept away.
"Now for that sweet grass,"
said the big Billy Goat Gruff.

He went *trippity-trippity-trippity-trap* across the bridge and ran up the mountain.

The three Billy Goats Gruff grew
fat on the sweet grass.

And the ugly troll?

He was never seen again.

Hopscotch has been specially designed to fit the requirements of the National Literacy Strategy. It offers real books by top authors and illustrators for children developing their reading skills. There are 43 Hopscotch stories to choose from:

* hardback